A Christmas Departure

A Novella

—Small Town Christmas—
Book 5

❄ ❄ ❄

D. Allen

DN Publishing

A Christmas Departure
Small Town Christmas, Book 5

Batavia, NY

www.DavidNethBooks.com

ISBN: 978-1-945336-05-8
First Edition

Subscribe to the author's newsletter for updates and exclusive content:
DavidNethBooks.com/Newsletter

Follow the author at:
www.facebook.com/DavidNethBooks
www.twitter.com/DavidNethBooks
www.instagram.com/DavidNethBooks

Also by D. Allen

Montana Beach

Summer Stay

Summer Job

Summer Nights

Small Town Christmas

A Christmas Reunion

A Christmas Charade

A Christmas Spark

A Christmas Song

A Christmas Departure

Standalone

Snow After Christmas

December 23rd
Tara

❄ ❄ ❄

2:00 P.M.

"United Coverage Insurance, this is Tara, how may I help you?"

My customer service voice sounds nothing like my regular speaking voice. I don't know the girl who comes out on the phone. Sometimes I even find myself playing with my hair when I talk to help me fit into character. Blech.

"You denied my claim and I had a perfectly good case!" a older woman's voice says breathlessly. No doubt the elevator music playing while she was on hold had done nothing to calm her anger. "There's no reason I shouldn't have been approved. I need you to fix this."

Another angry customer, oh joy. Merry Christmas to me.

"Okay, let me collect some information from you and I'll pull up your account so I can better assist you." Shifting the phone to my other ear, I prop it up with my shoulder, tilting my neck to keep it in place. "Please state your first and last name."

"Donna Goodman." She breaks into a phlegmy cough, but doesn't pull away from the phone enough so I have the pleasure of hearing her hack it up right in my ear. "That's G-O-O-D-M-A-N."

"And the last four of your social?"

She recites it and I verify her address and phone number to further confirm her identity.

"Okay, is this about the claim you submitted on the first of December?" I ask, looking at the few claims on her file.

"Yes, I was rear-ended and my neck hasn't been the same since," she says. "I've been to a *specialist* about it and he charges out the nose! I *thought* I'd be able to pay for that with my insurance claim from the car accident, but you people keep dragging your feet!"

"Well, it says here the car accident you filed the claim for happened in September," I say, reading from her account. "Unfortunately, we have a strict sixty-day policy, which would have expired the third week of November."

"That's only one week!" Donna barks on the other end, causing me to pull the phone away from my ear briefly. "This is a scam! I'm paying you people to support me when I need it!"

"I'm sorry, ma'am, but if the claim was filed within that sixty-day period, it would've been covered."

“One week! I’m calling the state and reporting you. This is ridiculous!”

“Well, ma’am, I’m sorry you feel that way. Let me look through your account and see if there’s any other way I can help you.” Clicking over to her policy plan, I skim through it and nothing jumps out at me. “Okay, other than the delay in the claim, it seems to qualify under your plan. Let me check one other thing. Ah, here it is. It looks like the last premium payment we have from you was from August.”

“Oh.” Donna’s voice is small.

“Since we haven’t received payment in several months, your account has been dormant. It says here that we’ve sent several notices to your address and have made phone calls.”

“Yeah…”

“They were sent to the address you verified at the start of this call. Did you receive those?”

“Yeah, I got the notices…”

“So unless those premiums were paid on time, you wouldn’t be covered under your United Coverage plan, unfortunately. If you were able to come up with the money from September through now, plus an additional ten percent surcharge fee, we would be able to backdate your coverage and maybe even accept your claim.”

“I don’t have that kind of money,” she says. “I lost my job in September and because of the accident I needed to pay to get my car fixed and while that was in the shop, I had a hard time finding a new job. By time I did, I could only get one that didn’t pay as much as my last one, so money’s been tight. And there's the holidays. Is there any way I can maybe do a payment plan?"

"You could submit an application, but since your account shows missed payments from September through now, it is very likely the claim would be denied."

"Oh."

I glance at the time on the phone and see that I've already been on with her for ten minutes. I have now officially reached the company policy quota of how long I should spend with a customer to make them feel important. "I'm sorry, ma'am. Is there anything else I can help you with?"

"You could help me figure out how to make Christmas happen for my kids," she says. "And while you're at it, you could help me figure out a way to make the mortgage payment so we're not homeless. This is ridiculous."

"I understand and I'm sorry for the stress this has caused you so close to the holidays, but unfortunately until we receive payment, there's nothing else we can do about your claim. Is there anything else I could help you with today?"

"Oh. Okay. No, that's all I needed, I guess."

"If you're interested, we could discuss bundling options with your homeowners insurance and auto insurance. That might bring down the total cost."

"No, that's okay."

"Well, I thank you for calling United Coverage Insurance and I hope you have a very merry Christmas and a happy New Year."

"You too," she murmurs.

I hang up the phone and write up a summary of the call and my explanation for how the situation was handled. All around my cubicle, phones ring and my colleagues talk to other customers in their own fake customer service voices.

When I first started, telling people I couldn't help them used to bother me. After four years working in insurance, I've grown accustomed to giving people bad news. Even a little calloused to it. I'm not happy about it or proud of it, but it's my job.

After hanging up the phone with Donna, I punch out for my lunch and head to the break room. It's late for lunch, but that's the way I like it. Going on my break after the lunch rush gives me time away from my coworkers, meaning I don't have to make small talk, which is the last thing I want to do after using my fake customer service voice all day.

Not that anyone would try to strike up a conversation with me. I've been here long enough. I've made my feelings on the matter known: Tara does not make friends.

Sitting in the dank, sticky break room, I revel in the silence. Sure, I can hear the hubbub of activity going on just outside the door, but none of that is happening in my world right in this room. Closing my eyes, I lean back and take a moment to be still and just breathe. A moment where nothing is expected of me and nobody is calling to complain about their problems. A moment that is purely mine.

My phone buzzing on the table snatches all of that away.

Jumping, I grab it quickly and let out a groan when I see it's my mother. She does not know how to keep conversations short.

"Hi Ma," I say.

"Why hello!" she says in her usual perky tone. "How is my favorite daughter doing?"

I know why she's calling: I still haven't given her an answer about whether I'm coming home for Christmas, even though I made the decision to just stay in Chicago weeks ago.

"I'm fine," I tell her.

"Work keeping you busy?"

I might not have to deal with small talk from my coworkers, but I still can't escape it from my mother. Telling her to cut to the chase is not going to fly with her. For the same reason that I haven't told her my Christmas plans yet: I don't have the heart to break hers.

"Yeah, the usual end-of-the-year claim calls. How's everything back home?" "Home" being Batavia, the little city in New York where I grew up and promptly left as soon as I could. College was my saving grace.

"Good. Your dad's shoulder's been bothering him. He can't hardly lift anything no more. We have an appointment with the doctor on New Year's Eve, I believe." She chuckles. "Hey! A rhyme! I do it all the time!"

As she continues to laugh, I can only muster a faint smile. I don't know how she continues to be so happy-go-lucky.

I glance at the clock and say, "Look, Mom, I'm going

to have to get back to work soon."

"Oh, well, before you go I just called to ask you if you were planning on coming home for Christmas this year."

I sigh, which apparently is answer enough for her.

"Oh *please*! You haven't been home in two years and we miss you. There's always an empty space at the table for you."

"Mom, I haven't booked a flight and Christmas is in two days."

"I'm sure there's still flights available. You have two airport options to fly out of and two options to fly into."

"Two? Nothing flies to Rochester, Mom." One of the perks of Batavia is that it's between Buffalo and Rochester, which each has its own airport. If luck was really on my side, I'd even have Niagara Falls to fly into, but only a few airlines fly there and it's even farther to my mom's house.

"You can decide which airport when you look for a flight home."

"I was planning on stopping into the office tomorrow morning to finish up a few things."

"Work can wait," she says. "Your family can't. Not when we don't know how many more Christmases we're going to have together."

My heart drops at that. Mom's had cancer in the past. Twice. Thankfully she went into remission both times. Perhaps that's part of the reason why I like to keep my distance in Chicago. Maybe then it won't hurt as much when my parents do eventually go.

"Tad and Sherry will be there with the baby."

My brother and his wife live in Buffalo and it's only about a forty-five minute drive to my mother's house. He's a teacher, so it's not like he needs to worry about taking time off of work. Other than visiting with Sherry's family, which they usually do on Christmas Eve, he has no other commitments for the holidays. He can manage to drive out to my parents' for Christmas.

But a last-minute flight? I'm not sure I can swing that.

Mom's right, though. It has been two years since I've been home at all. I'm due for a visit. And I do miss them. I miss home, even with all of its small town shortcomings.

"Okay," I say with another sigh. "I'll see what I can find for flights."

"Oh, yay!" Mom cheers. "I'm so happy to hear that!"

"Don't get your hopes up," I add quickly. "There are still a lot of ifs. Like the flights to Buffalo might be booked or they might just cost way too much."

"Your father and I will pay the difference if it costs too much," she says. "Consider it a Christmas gift. Actually, we'll pay for the whole flight, regardless the cost. We just want to see you, sweetie."

I smile. "I want to see you too."

"Well, look into those flights and let me know! You don't have much time left!"

❄ ❄ ❄

6:00 P.M.

"WHAT ARE YOU still doing here?" Angel, the evening janitor, asks when she comes to collect my trash.

"Finishing up some last-minute things that I had planned to do tomorrow." I snatch a piece of paper from the printer, add it to a manilla folder and store it in the drawer of my desk.

Angel pulls out my trash and ties it off. "You doing anything fun for the holidays?"

"Looks like I'm going home." I open a new tab and Google flights from Chicago to Buffalo.

"I bet your mom's real happy about that." She waves a new bag in the air to fluff it out before setting it in the trash bin.

"Very much so. She offered to pay for the flight." No flights from Midway to Buffalo tonight or tomorrow. Nothing until the day after Christmas.

"Girl, you gotta go then!" she says with a laugh.

"That's what I'm working on." I didn't want to go to O'Hare tomorrow, but if that's the only option. Changing the airport preferences, I search for flights from O'Hare to Buffalo.

"You have a merry Christmas," she says. "I'll see you when you get back!"

"You too, Angel. Thanks." My eyes don't leave my computer screen as the results populate. American Airlines, United, Delta, none of them have any available flights for December 24th from Chicago to Buffalo. At either of Chicago's airports.

Groaning, I reach for my phone to type out the text to my mother explaining the bad news when I decide to click on the option to include nearby airports in my search.

When the results populate, I jump up with surprise when I see an available one for tomorrow morning at 10:00. As I add the flights to my cart and begin the checkout process, I click on the details of the flight and see two strikes against it.

Strike One: It's flying out of O'Hare. One of the busiest airports in the country on one of the busiest travel days of the year.

Strike Two: It's flying into Rochester. One of the smallest airports and one that nobody in my family knows how to get to.

With no other options, I finish the sale and purchase my tickets before they are bought by someone else.

Looks like I'm flying to Rochester tomorrow.

December 23rd
Peter

❄ ❄ ❄

7:00 P.M.

Much to my chagrin, I'm much more breathless than I'd like to admit when I finally make it to the bar on West Madison Street in Chicago's West Loop neighborhood. It took me a bus, a train ride, and an Uber to get here, but I made it. My heavy duffel bag slung over my shoulder with a few clothes, my camera, and some lighting equipment weighs me down.

Unfortunately, that's not the true reason for my breathlessness.

Swinging open the door into the hip new bar, I walk in and try to keep my composure. The publisher of *Chi-Life* magazine has booked the entire place for the staff Christmas party. Mr. Roper, the editor-in-chief and the one who hired me for this job, said I could find him here if I didn't make it to the office by 6:00. Technically, that was my deadline. He's cut me some slack in the past, so I'm hoping he will again.

Of course, I've never been an *hour* late with the photos he's hired me to take.

The place is decked out in holiday cheer. From the garland curled around the exposed metal joists above to the clear lights in the window and even to the red bows and wreathes hung up on the brick wall, it's hard to forget that it's two days before Christmas. Not only that, but most people are dressed in some sort of red or green. Evidently nobody was brave enough to wear an ugly Christmas sweater. Not in a professional setting anyway.

Meandering through the crowd of unfamiliar faces, I track Mr. Roper down at the bar. I hear him before I see him. I even smell him before my eyes spot him. Clearly, he's been here for a while. A part of me wonders if I would've even caught him at the office had I been ready by 6:00.

"Helpern!" he shouts when he sees me with his glassy eyes. His voice is husky, garbled. Like he constantly has phlegm in his throat. It doesn't help that the pounding music makes my ears ring. "There you are! It's about time!" A true man of power, he's surrounded by five other men who aspire to be just as powerful as him and therefore sneer at me just as he is to earn even an ounce of his respect. Too bad being his puppy-dogs won't make any of them stand out.

"Yes, I'm sorry, sir," I start. "The model you put me in contact with was late and then I had to set up the lighting—"

"I don't want to hear excuses," he says. "For someone who's last name starts with 'Help,' you haven't been much of one with this project."

His groupies chuckle around us.

"I'm sorry, sir, but if you'd let me ex—"

"Do you even have the pictures?"

Fishing in my pocket, I retrieve the memory card. "Here they are."

Roper takes it from me and slides it into his shirt pocket. "You know what this tardiness means, don't you?"

I force myself to stare directly at him and none of the other jeering fools around him.

"I'm going to have to go into the office tomorrow to upload these," he says. "*If* they're even any good."

"Sir, I've done shoots for *Chi-Life* before. You've seen the work I do. You can trust the quality of it."

"Ha!" he snorts. "I can't trust you! You can't even show up on time!"

"Sir, I said I was sorry for that. There were factors out of my control that—"

He reaches around and pulls out his wallet his back pocket. "Here's something in *my* control. We agreed on $200 an hour, right?"

I nod. "Yes, and it was two hours' worth of work."

"I'll tell you what, this hour that you're late is coming out of your pay. So you only get an hour's pay. But lucky for you, it's tax-free!" He throws two fifties above my head and they float down to the floor. He chuckles with the rest of his cronies as I quickly snatch them up.

"Merry Christmas to you too," I murmur.

Roper waves me away, like a servant who's done his bidding. "Now get out of here, Helpern. You're not actually a *Chi-Life* employee so this party is not for you."

Biting my tongue, I turn and start walking to the door, hearing one of his groupies call out, "Bye!" from behind me and then start laughing.

Living the dream, one freelance job at a time.

❄ ❄ ❄

9:00 P.M.

AFTER BEING ON my feet all day, it feels incredible to finally fall back onto a nice, warm, comfortable bed. A bed that cost me nearly as much as I just made two hours ago, but that's what I get for not booking a room ahead of time—not that I know where I'm going to be most nights.

Despite how good this bed feels, I force myself to get up and take a shower. I'm probably filthy, having spent most of the day walking around the streets of Chicago, the last bit of which I spent anxiously trying to find a room to stay in for the night. This room—a deluxe suite—was the only available one left in the area, unless I wanted to fork over more money to take my chances in another part of the city. Of course, they don't just slap "deluxe" on the name for aesthetic. It comes with a cost.

As much as I hate spending all this money on one room for one night—realistically less than twelve hours—

I'm going to take full advantage of these amenities as best I can, starting with the jet shower head, the plush towels, and the soft bathrobe.

Taking a seat in the small living room area in the bathrobe after my shower, I call my dad back. He called me earlier when I was in the desperate hunt for a hotel room and I didn't have the time—or the energy—to hold up a conversation.

Even though it's nearly 10:30 back in New York, I still call him back.

It rings and rings and rings and rings before he finally picks up.

"Peter?"

"Dad, hi. Sorry it's so late. I finally got a room and I wanted to take a shower first."

"It's okay. So you're settled for the night?"

"Yeah, I'm too beat to go anywhere." I play with the end of the tie for the bathrobe, running the fabric between my fingers.

"Long day?"

"Every day's a long day."

He chuckles. "But you're busy, right?"

"Yeah, for the most part."

"Busy's good."

"Yeah."

"Well, listen," Dad finally says after the small talk, "I called earlier because your mother wanted me to double check that you're still coming tomorrow."

"Wouldn't miss it."

"We miss you and we can't wait to see you."

"Believe me, it'll be nice to be home. I pretty much have the rest of this week off and the next few weeks I have jobs lined up in Rochester, so I'll be staying pretty local."

Rochester, only about an hour away from Batavia, where my parents live and where I grew up. It's my "home base," if I can even say I have one. I travel so much for different freelancing jobs that I'm paying for an apartment I'm barely ever in.

"Your mother will be glad to hear that you're going to be home for a while," he says. "She's already gone up to bed. I was about to head up there myself and I must've dozed off."

"You should get to bed, then. I'm probably going to do the same here shortly."

"I will. You have a good night."

"You too, Dad. Love you." I start to pull the phone away, but I hear him ask another question. Very typical of Dad. Doesn't know how to end a phone call.

"What time does you flight come in tomorrow?"

"It leaves O'Hare at 10:00 tomorrow and it's an hour and a half flight, so factoring in the time change, I should get into Rochester around 12:30 your time."

"You said you're flying into Rochester?"

I run my hands through my damp hair, trying to squelch my annoyance from having to repeat the same information I've told them a thousand times already, the last of which was only ten seconds ago. "Yes."

"Okay. Keep us posted. Do you want us to pick you

up? We might even be able to get Tori to come too."

Tori, my older sister, who still lives in Batavia and probably has a much closer relationship to my parents than I do with all of my traveling.

"I left my car there, so I'll be fine."

"You left it in the airport parking? That's going to cost a fortune!"

"Dad, I do it all the time. I kind of have to. I'm there at least once a month, if not more."

"Yeah, I suppose."

"All right, I'm going to get some sleep."

"I should too," he says.

"I'll see you tomorrow. I can't wait."

"Me neither, son. Be safe and let us know when you're leaving and all that."

"I will."

"Okay," he says with an exaggerated sigh. "I'll let you go."

"All right, Dad."

"Good night, son. Love you."

"Love you too. Good night."

When I end the call, I pull up Facebook and scroll through, too lazy to get up and go to bed. I see a post from my sister of her new singing video with her boyfriend Isaac, covering "Baby, It's Cold Outside." They've been posting videos together for the last year and have been slowly gaining followers. It's something Tori's been trying to do for a while, so it's very cool to see it actually coming to life.

The last time I talked to her, she was very excited

about how much their YouTube channel has grown since it started. She's even developed a newfound appreciation for her job at the high school, although I'm sure Isaac's partnership has helped with that too.

After the video ends, I click on another one of them. This one for a duet version of an Adele song. Then I click another, and another, and another. Before I know it, it's 11:30 and I can barely keep my head up.

Closing the apps on my phone, I get up, click off the lights, and go to bed. One more day of traveling tomorrow and then I'll be stationary for a while.

Traveling on Christmas Eve was not my first choice, but it's what I'm going to have to do. Hopefully it goes smoothly without any bumps in the road.

December 24th

Tara

❄ ❄ ❄

8:00 A.M.

Two hours until the flight leaves and I'm still stuck in traffic just outside the airport. Sitting in the back of the Uber, I try to get lost in my book, but my mind keeps worrying about whether I'm going to make it in time. I like to arrive at the airport three hours before the flight leaves, which means I'm already an hour late.

That's not my fault.

I woke up at 5:00, called for an Uber to arrive by 6:00—knowing that it would take about forty-five minutes to get to the airport. The driver had a hard time finding my apartment and by time he finally stopped, got my bags loaded, and we set off, it was nearly 6:30.

Turns out the holiday traffic caused more of a delay than I thought it would, even with the early wake-up time, and now we're currently waiting to change lanes on the I-190 into O'Hare, along with about a million other cars. To add to all of that, it's been snowing pretty good since I left my apartment. With the number of cars already on the road, all of that snow is just turning to slush and causing even further delays.

I should've just taken the train.

Of course, that would have also required me to take an Uber to the appropriate line. My apartment is close to the line that takes me to work downtown, but not a lot of other places in the city. One of the detriments of where I live.

Turning back to my mystery novel, I try to focus on the detective interrogating the suspect, but I'm pulled out of the book when the driver hits the brakes hard and slams on his horn.

"That jerk just cut me off!"

"Sorry for making you drive in all of this," I murmur. Not only am I stressing out about potentially missing my flight, but I'm also feeling guilty about adding to the traffic nightmare when there was a much more sensible alternative, in terms of people involved. The train probably would've taken just as long, if not longer, but it would've meant one less car on the road.

"Don't worry, ma'am," he says. "I decided to drive this morning, not you. I simply answered your call."

"Well, I appreciate it. Thank you." I settle back in with my book and try to focus.

Apparently my apology in response to his outburst

was enough to calm him because he's quiet the rest of the way to the airport.

When we finally pull up to the departures drop offs, I point to the first spot I see, even though it's the furthest from the main door.

"Right here is fine," I tell him. "I can walk."

"Are you sure?"

"Positive." I unbuckle my seatbelt as he pulls up. The car has barely come to a stop before I open my door and step out.

A moment later, he joins me at the back of the car to unload my suitcase. To our left, cars, taxis, and other Ubers whiz by us in an effort to get a closer spot, sending snow and slush flying in all directions. I just want to get inside where it's dry and warm, trying not to think of the fact that if it hadn't have been for my mother's guilt trip, I would be nice and warm in my cubicle at the office right now.

"Thanks again." I slip him a twenty. "I really appreciate it. Merry Christmas."

"Merry Christmas to you too! And thank you!"

I wave him goodbye and start power-walking among the other holiday travelers under the covered awning to the main entrance. Luckily, the slushy mess is minimal under the covered walkway.

As I get closer to the door, I become more and more anxious as the crowd around me seems to grow. Everyone is on a mission to get home in time for the holidays and most people don't mind cutting out the holiday cheer to be the first in line or first one through the door.

Finally, I make it inside and get in the queue for my airline to check my bags. While I wait, I fill out the tag information to secure to my bags and write out a text to my mom.

Checking my bags at the airport now. Then it's through security and waiting for the flight.

Two minutes later, I get a response: *What time does the flight leave?*

I told her this just last night, but still I type out my reply. My parents are my ride home from the airport once I land.

10:00. We should arrive in Rochester around 12:30ish.

Ok.

I check the time: 8:45. Assuming security doesn't take forever, I should still be okay. I'm cutting it closer than I'd like, but I suppose it's not the end of the world. I'll still make it home in time.

My stomach growls and my back is already stiff from standing and waiting. It's going to be a long day.

When I'm called up, the airline worker tosses my bag on the conveyor belt behind them and I show them my ID and take my plane ticket, then I get in the long line for security.

Once again, I type out another text to my mother.

Just got in line for security.

Five minutes later, my phone buzzes with another text.

K.

Even though I know she doesn't realize that a one

letter response—especially *that* letter—is a surefire way to tell someone you're pissed off via text, my initial reaction is a bristled one. But I let it go. Mom has no idea. She's probably cooking up a storm getting ready for the family to come over tomorrow. I wonder what she has planned for us tonight. I try not to let myself get excited, but it's hard.

When I was growing up, we used to go to my grandparents' house on Christmas Eve with my aunts and uncles and cousins. They lived in a big house on East Avenue and could hold all of us. But they passed away shortly after I graduated high school. At that point, the aunts and uncles were getting older and didn't like driving so late in the snow and the cousins were all growing up and moving on to college and other careers.

Myself included. I went to college in Cleveland before landing my first job in Toledo and eventually moving to Chicago. With each new venture, I keep moving west.

Up ahead, one of the TSA guards opens a new queue and waves me through as the first in line. Once again, I show my ID before stepping forward to the security checkpoint. With a growing number of people behind me, I unload as fast as I can. Opening my bag, I pull out my electronics, taking off my belt, shoes, and jacket and stuff them into a gray plastic crate.

I don't envy people who do this regularly. And the regulars in the next lines over are obvious. They move with such efficiency and confidence that they seem to breeze through security in no time.

When the next guard waves me forward for the full-body scan, I stand with my hands above my head as they search me for the weapons that I don't have.

Somehow, though, they see something they don't like and they ask me to "please step aside."

"Ma'am, please stand with your legs shoulder-width apart and your arms out," a female TSA guard says.

I comply and wait nervously as she waves the wand over me. Meanwhile, the people behind me pass through the security checkpoint and collect their things, pushing the crates with my belongings to the side where things like my wallet or my phone could be snatched up without much notice. My anxiety builds, only worsened by the unwanted attention I'm receiving from the guards and the passing travelers.

The wand dings around my stomach.

The guard leans in closer to me and says, "Unfortunately, I'm going to need to do a more thorough search. We can do it right here or go somewhere private if that's what you'd prefer."

"Just a pat down?" I ask.

She nods.

I glance over to my belongings and say, "Here's fine."

As more people continue to pass through the security line around us, the guard pats down each of my limbs before deeming that I'm not a safety risk and allowing me to proceed.

Hallelujah.

Collecting my things, I pull myself together and pull out my phone. 9:15. Not too bad. The worst is behind me.

Now all I need to do is find the right terminal and the correct gate.

I send another text to my mom telling her I got through security okay. She doesn't need to know that I got an early Christmas "gift" from the TSA guard.

With my carry-on bag slung over my shoulder and the rest of my belongings in their rightful place, I follow the crowd that's heading toward Terminal 3 and make the trek through the enormous airport. Checking the time again, I decide I can spare a few minutes getting something to eat in one of the horribly overpriced airport convenience stores.

Predictably, the store is packed. I thought one of the stores closer to my specific gate wouldn't be as busy but alas, I was wrong. As I select my snacks for the plane, a woman steps beside me to look at the same options. Her son—who can't be anymore than eight years old—follows her with a book in his hand that he presumably got off the stand, judging from the sticker on the back of it.

"Put that away, Jackson," she says. "It's too expensive."

"In a minute, Mama, it's just starting to get good."

I notice he's only a few pages in and I smirk. I like his determination, but also wonder if he's actually reading the book. I've seen enough temper tantrums in stores to know that sometimes it's less about the thing itself than it is about getting *something* new.

Grabbing a trail mix and some jerky, I get in line for the register. I grab an oversized bottle of water along the way. As I wait, I notice the mother pull one thing after another off the shelf just to check the price and put it back.

I can relate. Traveling is expensive enough and the way they overprice everything once you're in the airport only makes it worse. And buying for two? I can't imagine.

Finally, she settles on a single bottle of water and a small bag of gummies.

"Come on, sweetie." She waves her hand to get him to take it, but he's too focused on the book to notice. Looks like it's one of the Diary of Wimpy Kid books. "Put that away. I don't have enough for it."

"Mom, please! I'm really going to read it!"

"Maybe ask Santa for it," she says with a sigh.

"There's no time! He's coming tonight and that's even *if* we make it to Uncle Eddie's by then."

"Jackson, I said no. Now put it back so nobody thinks you're trying to steal it." She gets in line behind me and adjusts her purse as she watches her son, who moves across the store back toward the books, his eyes latched on the pages of the book the whole time.

The woman gives me a polite smile and I open my mouth to offer to pay for it, but the cashier calls me forward before any of the words can come out.

As I lay my items on the counter, I decide it's probably for the best. People who don't have a lot of money tend to be very proud. And although I just want to give that little boy an opportunity to read a book, I also don't want to insult the mother. Not when tensions are already high in an airport. On Christmas Eve.

"That'll be twenty-three fifty," the cashier tells me.

Sighing, I pull out my card and slide it. Hopefully I

won't have too many more of these purchases before I get home. The flight leaves in about half an hour. Once I'm on the plane, it's smooth-sailing until I'm home.

After the cashier hands me my receipt and I tuck it firmly in my wallet, I collect my purchases and head out toward Gate L6A.

December 24th
Peter

❄ ❄ ❄

9:00 A.M.

My duffel bag bounces off my back as I race along the crowded platform of the train. Sweat drips down my face and along my spine under my layers of winter clothes as I weave between people, feeling the hot breeze of the stopping trains and the venting of the building above.

The last stop on the Blue Line is right at the airport. It was a hell of a commute that involved walking several blocks to the closest train stop, taking a train downtown, only to board another train out to the airport, which stopped at too many stations on the way.

But I've finally made it.

Now if only I can actually get into the airport, through security, and to my gate in time to catch my flight by 10:00. If I don't get on this plane, I'm out of money for another one. And even if I could afford one, the likelihood of me booking another flight for today are slim. I need to get going.

I'm slowed by the crowd when I make it to the staircase leading up to the airport and I shuffle among other disgruntled travelers looking to get through the checkpoints and to their planes on time. It's not ideal, but traveling is something I've grown accustomed to with my freelance photography jobs.

Of course, I try not to be in such a rush like I am right now.

The trouble is, in the chaos of getting the pictures to Mr. Roper in time and finding a hotel room for the night, I forgot to set my alarm for this morning. Meaning that when the sun finally woke me up at about 7:30, I had enough time to use the bathroom, brush my teeth, and throw my few belongings into my bag.

Luckily, I travel light, so I don't have to worry about checking my bags. That is, if I ever get *into* the airport.

When the elderly lady in front of me finally scales the final step of the stairs, I step around her and wait in line for the self-service kiosks to print my boarding pass.

Checking the time again, I see it's 9:17. I need to get going. Security is going to take forever. And there's probably no way I'm stopping anywhere to grab any sort of breakfast. I'm a little lightheaded from lack of food. I haven't eaten anything since about 4:30 yesterday. Another hazard of freelance work.

When it's my turn at the kiosk, I punch in the number for my ticket, verify my information, and wait for it to print.

The machine barely spits it out before I snatch it and run to the security line, which doesn't look promising. Another time check: 9:25.

Not good.

The security line seems to inch forward, but I finally make it to the front of one of the lines and plop my bag into a bin, spilling over the electronic contents in the next bin over. My shoes, belt, wallet, and phone go into a third bin and I wait anxiously for the line to proceed.

The gentleman passing through the security scanner in front of me is told to step forward and back, forward and back at least two times before he's permitted to proceed. Meanwhile, I glance up at the nearest clock and see it's just about 9:40.

They've probably already started boarding the plane.

When it's my turn to step through, I pass by with no issues and quickly collect my things from the bins, shoving everything back into my bag. My feet jam into my shoes and I pull the laces tight and then quickly tie them. Folding my belt in my hand, I throw my bag over my shoulder and grab my jacket with my free hand and take off in a run toward Terminal 3.

Less than twenty minutes until the plane leaves.

"Excuse me! Excuse me!" I call out as I work my way through the large throngs of people meandering lazily along the corridor.

Reaching around, I hike up the back of my pants, falling because the belt is in my hand and not around my waist. I probably look like a crazy person but at the moment

I don't care. And I don't have the time to reloop my belt properly.

I reach Terminal 3 and am immediately struck with the vast amount of decorations filling the terminal. I half wonder if there were decorations throughout the whole airport that I missed before.

I don't give it much more thought than that and I sprint down the corridor, weaving between groups of people, nearly taking out a woman with a stroller.

She shouts, "Hey!"

I throw a "Sorry!" over my shoulder and keep going, only slowing slightly when I finally see Gate L6A.

It's empty. Only the airline gate agent remains, typing away at her computer. But the door to the jetway is still open.

Nearly colliding with the desk to come to a stop, I drop my bag beside me, my shoulder aching from its weight, and ask breathlessly, "Are…you…still…boarding?"

"Are you on this flight to Rochester, New York?"

I nod and start to hook my belt through the belt loops, doing my best to calm my breathing so I don't look *totally* insane.

She eyes me as I redress, but apparently decides to ignore it. "Can I see your boarding pass? They're going to pull away from the gate shortly." She reaches for her walkie and raises it to her mouth. "Hold on, we have one last-minute passenger." She raises an eyebrow at me as I finish hooking my belt and then pull my crumpled ticket out of my pocket, where I stashed it after security.

She flattens it and it takes a couple tries before she's able to scan it.

"Peter Helpern?"

"That's me."

"You're all set to board. Unfortunately, with the late boarding, you'll have to find the first available seat, but there will be one available for you. Please enjoy your flight."

Tossing on my jacket, I throw my bag over my opposite shoulder and speed-walk down the jetway. Even though I know I no longer need to hurry, it's still hard to kick the feeling of urgency.

A flight attendant greets me at the door of the plane. "Welcome! Watch your step." She points her arm down the aisle of the plane. "Please find an empty seat."

Quickly scanning the rows in front of me, I try to tell myself to relax. I'm on the plane and I'm ready to go. No need to worry about arriving on time anymore. But my heart is still racing, even as relief washes over me.

Spotting an empty seat, I toss my bag in the overhead compartment and sit. Pulling out my phone, I type a quick text to my parents, telling them I've boarded before putting it on airplane mode.

I let out a deep breath and lean back against the seat. Noticing the woman sitting to my right, I look over to introduce myself and get a good look at her face for the first time.

"Oh. Tara. Hi."

DECEMBER 24TH
Tara

❄ ❄ ❄

10:00 A.M.

Offering a polite smile to Peter, I reply, "Hi."

With everyone else on the plane already settled, I spotted him the moment he walked on and instinctively let out an audible groan. I managed to stifle a second one when he chose the empty seat beside me to sit his no-good rear-end in.

"How've you been?" he asks with a smile. His sandy blond hair hangs down over his forehead and as he lifts his arm to brush it out of the way, I get a whiff of him and am reminded of our entire history.

I let out a sigh and take him in. "I'm all right."

He has a few more tattoos than the last time I saw him. Just little ones along his forearms. Words, little doodles, a few birds. It looks like he drew all over himself.

"It's been a while," he says.

"That it has."

"We're talking—what?—like five, six years?" he asks.

"Something like that." As much as I don't want to talk to him, the fact of the matter is we're stuck on this plane together until we land in Rochester. I better keep the peace, otherwise it'll be a long two hours.

"Are you living out here now?" he asks.

"Yeah. Are you?" That would be just my luck. To move away from home only to end up in the same city as my ex. Despite its size, Chicago just isn't big enough for both of us.

"Nah," he says, still flashing those perfect teeth. "Technically I live in Rochester, but since I'm a freelance photographer, I'm never really there."

"Nice," I say with very little enthusiasm. I'm not doing too well at keeping the peace, so I add, "You've always wanted to do that."

"Yeah, and it's been a wild ride. I've been all over the world. Shanghai, Tokyo, Paris, LA, you name it. I've done everything from portraits to covers to promotional shoots and all in between. I've met some *incredible* people and have some crazy stories. I could talk all day about them…"

And he does.

For what seems like forever, Peter rambles on, detailing—and, I'm sure, exaggerating—different stories from his travels. How he lost his luggage in Thailand but didn't have time to reclaim it before his flight to Greece, so he went two weeks with only the bag on his back. Or how he tried hookah for the first time in Lithuania. Or how he snapped a great shot of a lion mauling a gazelle in Central Africa, only to narrowly escape with all his limbs intact.

Individually, these are all great stories and great experiences. But clumped together and told to someone you haven't talked to in years is a bit much.

"...since it was Brazil, it was so hot and I needed a shower and a change of clothes, but I didn't have time to run back to my hostel and change. Not to mention, I didn't even have a nice shirt to change into—"

"Mm-hmm," I murmur, deciding to interrupt him because I can't stand the stories anymore. "I've been to Brazil. It's beautiful there. I went with a couple friends right after college. You know, Maisy and Talia?" He better remember those girls. Not that I really talk to them much anymore.

"Oh yeah! Where'd you guys stay?"

"Rio de Janeiro." I leave out the part about staying at a resort and only being there for the beach. At least the conversation has shifted off of him for a bit.

"Oh, that's a tourist town," he says dismissively. "You should've gone inland more. Brasilia was my favorite, but Rio was nice too."

And just like that, the conversation is back on him. I give up trying to talk about myself because what's the point? I can deal with a miserable plane ride home. Once we land, I won't ever have to see him again.

So I settle in for a long, exhausting ride and try to let my mind wander about anything else.

"...you would've thought it was another country," he goes on. This time about being out west or something. I've lost track. "My skin was on fire with sunburn, but if I covered up anymore I would've passed out from heat exhaustion. Or looked like a bum and then nobody would've picked me up on the side of the road. That'll teach you never to miss the bus, right?" He doesn't wait for my response before diving into the rest of his story. "So finally I get a car to stop and—"

"Good morning, everyone," the pilot's voice comes over the loudspeaker and I send up a silent Hail Mary as a thank you for putting an end to Peter's stories. "Sorry to keep you waiting for so long. We were working on de-icing the plane, but now we're just waiting for the go-ahead to get us up in the air. If you can look out the nearest window, there's some snow coming through for now. The forecast is saying it'll blow right by us and once it does, we'll be on our way. So sit tight and hopefully we'll get going soon."

There's a collective groan throughout the plane once he signs off, myself among them. I've had to endure the agony that is Peter's running mouth and we haven't even pulled away from the airport yet. Taking out my phone, I text my mother to tell her the bad news.

After I've sent the text, I can see Peter doing the same.

"My dad's anxious to get me home," he says. "Are you going to see your parents?"

"Oh, have you run out of things to say about yourself?"

He studies me, likely debating whether he should

return my snark or let it slide. Thankfully, he lets it go.

"Tara, I'm only trying to make conversation."

"Are you, though?" I can't help myself. "You've barely asked two questions about how I've been doing in the several years since we've last seen each other and *now* you want to have a conversation? You realize that conversations happen as a give and take, right? Meaning everyone involved is both talking and listening to what the other person is saying. And generally conversations are a pleasant exchange of information."

He shakes his head with a closed-mouth smile. "Funny. But I actually don't need to ask any questions because it's obvious you're still a cold bitch like you were back then. Guess some things don't change."

Several eyes turn to us as our voices rise, but my annoyance keeps me going.

"Oh, you mean like how you're still a stuck-up brat who thinks the world should bow down to you because you're so *cultured*." I roll my eyes. "Give me a break."

"At least I've gone out and seen the world, Tara. Let me guess, you work in an office job doing data entry or something like that. Predictable, easy, *boring*."

"Well at least I don't need validation from complete strangers just to feel worthy," I fire back. "From where I'm standing, it looks like all these world travels of yours are really just a way for you to hide how empty and shallow you feel inside."

"You want to talk about shallow? What about how you're so quick to judge me for my lifestyle, but you were the one who had a chip on your shoulder from the moment I sat down?"

"Maybe because seeing you reminded me of everything you put me through the last time we spoke."

"That was six years ago," he says. "Can't you just move on?"

"Move on? You broke my heart!"

With that admission, I realize just how loud we've become and just how many people are shooting daggers at us. At me. With every flight, there's always that one annoying area of the plane. A baby crying. Someone chewing their food too loudly. Snoring. That odd odor. The armrest hog. Or someone who's arguing loudly, airing their dirty laundry for the world to hear.

That's me. I'm the nuisance. I'm the one making the bad situation of being stuck on a plane even worse. For everyone.

Hunkering lower in my seat, I turn to look out the window and watch the wind blow snow off the roof of the neighboring terminal and try to silently stifle my embarrassment.

Peter gets the hint too and plays around on his phone. After a few minutes, conversation around us picks back up and slowly we're not the focus of everyone's attention anymore.

Joy to the world.

Quietly, Peter says to me, "I'm sorry. I didn't mean to keep talking about myself. I didn't realize I was doing it and I certainly didn't want to fight with you."

I sigh heavily and try to think of the best response, but I just keep looking out the window.

"I know we both need to cool off, but I think we could use this time on the plane to talk things out," he offers. "Maybe running into each other here, of all places, is a sign that it's time to put to rest that moment of our lives." He pauses, waiting for me to respond. When I don't, he goes on. "I don't know. I just hate to go on thinking that we still haven't resolved everything."

I turn to him and say, "Peter, I really don't want to talk about it."

"Oh. Okay, sorry. I was just thinking, since we're both flying to Rochester and presumably we're both going home to Batavia to be with our families tomorrow, maybe we can carpool. I parked at the airport so there's already a ride waiting for us. And it would give us about another hour to talk things through—if you're ready for it, then. It's just a suggestion. I don't want to ruin your Christmas."

"Then please stop talking," I say.

He lets out an annoyed sigh, but finally does as I ask.

As I watch the snow blowing through the open airport runway, I let my mind wander back to those years I've buried deep down in the depths of my memories. The ones with Peter. The ones where I was happy and young, but naïve and innocent. The years and memories of my relationship with Peter tarnished by the ending.

Is he right? Could those bad feelings disappear with some closure? Could I look back at my relationship with him with a warm smile, instead of an overwhelming feeling of shame at being so stupid?

I'd like to believe that in the time that has passed, I've matured. That I've moved on. But have I really? My knee-jerk reaction to seeing Peter was to groan and snipe at him like a bratty teenager. If I really am better than that, then I need to be the adult here and extend the olive branch.

Turning back to him, I try to catch his attention, but he purposely keeps his eyes on his phone. Can't say I blame him with the way that I acted.

"Look, I'm sorry for everything I said," I tell him. "It shouldn't have come out like that. It's just a lot to process because I'm already not having a great day and I didn't expect to see you here and I took it all out on you. So I'm sorry."

He shrugs, his eyes still on his phone. "Okay."

I bite my top lip in an effort to keep anymore snark inside. Instead, I decide to answer some of the questions he asked earlier. "Anyway, yes, I am going home to see my parents for Christmas. I live out here now, Uptown Chicago. Been out here for probably about four years now. I work at an insurance company, so you were right about that, to an extent. I do process data in an office. But it affects people's lives, so it's kind of important, I guess."

I think back to Donna yesterday on the phone. I know for sure I ruined her Christmas, but I was only doing my job.

"So you're ready to talk to me, then?" He finally sets down his phone and looks up.

"I suppose, yes."

"So you'd talk to me if I just randomly called you up to make amends for those years and not just because we're stuck together on this plane for the unforeseeable future?"

"Peter, why are you making this more difficult?"

"Just answer the question."

"I don't know. You said it yourself, maybe seeing each other today is a sign."

"True, but what if the sign was me calling you out of the blue and not getting stuck on the plane with me? Are you really ready to make amends or are you just trying to pacify me to go on with our lives? Because I'm not interested in that. I want real conversation. Do you remember what that's like?"

I pull away and make a face. "Are you implying that I'm not normally genuine?"

"You work for an insurance company," he says, as if that explains it.

My voice grows as the annoyance builds again. "Well, at least I—"

"Ladies and gentlemen, this is your captain speaking again," a voice says from the speaker above us. "Looks like this snow squall is sticking around and we have no idea how long it's going to last. In an effort to make you as comfortable as possible, we're going to go ahead and de-board until the storm passes."

Everyone on the plane groans again and some people start springing up and pulling their belongings from the overhead compartments.

"Please be advised: this is *not* a cancellation. We are

simply de-boarding until the storm passes. We hope to be up and running in the next hour or so, but until then, I want to thank you for flying with us today."

December 24th
Peter

❄ ❄ ❄

2:00 P.M.

"We're still waiting for the weather to pass," I tell Dad over the phone. I'm pacing in the middle of the concourse, keeping an eye on my duffel bag still claiming my seat by the electrical outlets.

"Did they cancel it?"

"No, just delayed."

"See if you can get another flight out of there. Even to Buffalo."

"All of the flights in and out of O'Hare have been grounded," I tell him. "I bet Midway's the same. Besides, I don't really have the money to buy a second plane ticket."

I barely made it on this plane as it was, I think to myself.

"Don't worry about the money," he says. "Your mother and I just want you home."

"Thanks. I just don't know when that's going to happen."

"Get home as soon as you can," Dad says. "And keep us posted about how things are going over there. As of right now, the weather's fine here. Sunny, a little breezy, but not too bad. I guess we're supposed to get a couple inches overnight, but I don't think that's going to stop the plane from landing."

"Let's hope not."

"So what have you been doing since you got off the plane?"

"Just playing games on my phone," I say. "I think I'm going to take a walk, but I don't want to go too far in case they have us board again."

"I think you'll be fine. They have windows in the airport, don't they?"

I smile. "Yes, Dad, they do."

"So you can see if the weather's clearing up. I'm sure they'll make several announcements before the plane boards."

"True."

"Or you could even ask one of the ladies at the desk there."

I look up at the counter and notice it's a man standing there, typing something into the computer.

"Yeah, I could."

"Anyway, I know this isn't the best start to your Christmas, but try to make the most of it."

"I will, Dad. See you soon. Hopefully."

"Hopefully is right! Take care. Love you, son."

"Love you too." I end the call and slip my phone in my back pocket and turn back to the gate to look out the windows. The snow is still blowing off the roof, causing a whiteout and making it nearly impossible to even see the waiting airplane that we were on this morning.

Looking over, I see Tara sitting at a seat by the wall, a book in her lap and her eyes fixed intently upon it. Despite her casual demeanor, I can tell she's stressed. We're all stressed. Worried about whether we'll make it home in time. Annoyed that we're spending the first part of our holiday bored at an airport waiting for this act of God to pass.

That's the one thing that this diverse group has in common. All of us—whether we're black or white, young or old—are just trying to get somewhere to spend time with our loved ones for the holidays.

Looking around the room, I see just how tired people truly are, despite their activities that suggest otherwise. Just like Tara, each person waiting is keeping occupied in an effort to distract themselves from their worry about how long this flight will be delayed.

In one corner sits an older couple. The woman is talking on the phone while her husband reads a newspaper beside her. Across from them sits a man in a leather jacket and ripped jeans playing a game on his phone. Down the row is a mother and her son. The boy is probably around eight and doesn't seem to be able to sit still. Meanwhile, his mother tries to pull up videos on her phone, but with the number of people around, the internet connection is slow.

And then there's Tara, who's sitting quietly by herself, still reading that book. Despite the number of years that have passed, I still see the same girl I knew back in college: smart, reserved, but still a lot of fun. While still present, that girl is being hidden by this mask of responsibility and a skewed sense of maturity. I may not know Tara that well anymore, but I once did. And I hope she finds the happiness she deserves, because from where I'm standing, she doesn't look happy. Not like she was all those years ago.

Chancing a moment away from my bag, I go around the corner to the Starbucks and order two coffees. Starbucks might not be my favorite, but it's among the few options I have in the airport.

Carrying both cups over to Gate L6A, I take a seat next to Tara and extend one to her. "Here, I got this for you."

Her brow furrows as her eyes flick up to me. "What is it?"

I chuckle. "It's coffee, not arsenic."

She slips a bookmark in between the pages and sets the book aside before reaching for the cup.

"Honestly, I thought this would be a way to break the ice after our, um…*discussion* this morning."

"That's one way of sugarcoating it." She takes a careful sip.

"Um, if I recall, you were the one who had the loudest outburst."

Her eyes bug out and she turns to me. "Me!" She lowers her voice when several eyes look up at us. "You were the one who started it all."

"I'm not trying to point fingers here." I hold my free hand up as a sign of surrender. "I just thought I'd bring you some coffee to help make this wait not as boring."

She studies me and then settles back into her seat. "Well, thanks for this."

"Did I get it right?"

"Did you get what right?"

"Your order," I say. "I tried to remember the way you used to take it."

She takes another sip and then admits, "It's perfect. I'm kind of surprised you remembered."

"See? I'm not all bad."

Tara hooks an eyebrow. "Getting my coffee order right doesn't really make up for everything."

I force a smile. "You're really having a hard time letting your guard down, aren't you?"

"Why should I?"

"Because I'm trying here."

"Yeah, only because we ran into each other," she says. "Isn't that what you said to me this morning on the plane?"

"So you're saying I shouldn't even try to talk to you? That we should just pretend like we never knew each other?"

She looks down at her coffee and shrugs. "Maybe. I don't know."

Turning, I rest my foot on my knee and stare straight ahead. This did not go as well as I had hoped it would. I'm certainly not taking my father's advice about 'making the most' of being trapped here.

"Okay, so just tell me, what is it exactly that keeps you from letting the past stay in the past?" I finally ask. "Why are you so insistent on staying mad at me? What is it about me that ignites this deep-seated hatred in you?"

Tilting her head back, she looks me over. "You really want to know?"

I wave toward me and reposition myself so I'm facing her. "Yeah, come on. Lay it all out. What do we have to lose?"

"Okay." She sets her coffee cup down in the nearest cupholder and clasps her hands together. "How about when we were just reacquainted this morning, you wouldn't stop talking about yourself. Just like when we were younger and you broke up with me because I was graduating a year earlier than you."

"You were moving to—"

She puts up her hand. "Let me finish. Or how to this day you'd still rather travel the world than settle down anywhere."

"Since when is traveling a bad thing?"

"It is when you use it as an excuse to have a chip on your shoulder, acting like you're better than everyone else who hasn't seen the world because here in the *real world*, people can't always afford things like that. Or maybe they just have other priorities. But that would require you to think about other people and we've already established the fact that you don't. You haven't changed. You're still immature and that's not the type of person I care to spend my time with."

"Says the one who was quick to judge me from the moment you saw me step on that plane," I fire back. "You had your mind made up about me before I even opened my mouth and said a word. And if you think I have a chip on my shoulder, go ahead and take a look in the mirror because I only came over here to try to apologize for earlier."

"Real nice, deflecting all the blame onto other people," she says. "Once again, you're showing your immaturity. You might be able to navigate traveling the world, but try actually having a longstanding relationship with someone. I noticed there weren't any recurring people in your story. Honestly, who are you close to? A friend, a loved one, anyone? Someone who isn't a parent."

I open my mouth to respond, but I don't have a name to offer her. She's right that other than my family, I don't have any real friendships.

"Yeah, that's what I thought," she goes on. "And you cover up for it by talking about yourself, which only shows all of your insecurities."

"Well, if you've already made up your mind about me, there's nothing I can do to change that," I say. "You're going to think what you want. I've tried apologizing. I've tried making up for what happened several years ago, but you just won't let it go. We've been down this road before and it's getting us nowhere, so I'm just going to let you sit here and stew by yourself, because I'm sure that's all you really want to do."

Reaching over, I grab her coffee as I get to my feet.

"Hey, what are you doing?" she asks, reaching for it.

"This was a gift from me to you and since you want nothing to do with me, I thought I'd dispose of all traces of me from your life." I toss it in the nearest trash. "Have a nice flight and a merry Christmas. I really hope you do enjoy your time with your family. Maybe they can help you work out some of *your* insecurities."

She stares at me with the lower half of her jaw extended further than usual. I retake my seat across the gate, ignoring the few eyes that we've attracted. Our argument wasn't as loud as it was on the plane, but it certainly wasn't quiet either.

With my arms crossed, I glare at her with fury in my eyes. So much for making the most of the flight delay. Sorry Dad.

December 24th
Tara

❄ ❄ ❄

4:00 P.M.

"They claim we're still flying today, but this is getting ridiculous," I tell my mother over the phone. With my book finished, I decided to call her with the latest update just to give me something to do.

"How can they delay a plane that long?" she asks.

"I don't know, but I'm glad they're not canceling it." I pace along the windows overlooking the runway. Between the falling snow and the setting sun, I mostly just see my reflection in them. "I'd never get another flight home and I'd just be stuck here and this whole day would've been a waste."

"There aren't any other flights you can change to?"

"Not that I could find last night," I tell her. "To Rochester or Buffalo. And at this point, even if there was, it's probably already left for the night."

"Well, as long as you still have a flight, we'll still plan on you coming. I wish you were already here."

"Me too, Mom. Traveling like this for the holidays is really making me reconsider living in Chicago."

"You're moving back home?" she asks, excited.

"No, I was just saying, if I lived closer and could drive, this wouldn't be an issue. Like when I lived in Cleveland or Toledo, remember?"

"Oh. Right."

"Yeah."

"At least the flight isn't canceled, so you'll be home *sometime*," she says. "I just wish we knew when."

"I'll let you know as soon as I know something. Promise."

"Okay, dear. Hopefully it won't be too much longer. Love you."

"Love you too."

Locking my phone, I slide it in my pocket and look through the window, trying to see past my reflection. It's getting harder to see how much it's snowing, but it doesn't look like it's let up much. That's not a good sign.

As I make my way back to my seat, I try to come up with a positive alternative to not making it home. At least I'd save money on a plane ticket. I could catch up on some of my shows tomorrow. I might even be able to get a flight out for the weekend and we could celebrate a few days late. It wouldn't be the same but it'd be something.

Of course, if I stay home tomorrow, that means that all day I'll keep thinking about what I would be doing if I were home. From breakfast, to opening gifts, to visiting with family, to the festive turkey dinner my mom is probably already preparing, I'll miss it all. And that's not to mention the break from my routine that I know I desperately need more than I'll ever admit out loud. If I stay here in Chicago, December 25th will just seem like another day off. Nothing special.

A woman in an airline uniform steps to the desk and raises the phone receiver to her mouth. Everyone else sitting around the gate takes notice too.

Maybe this is the announcement we've been waiting for. Maybe the forecast is showing something different than I've been seeing all day. Maybe the snow is clearing enough for us to get in the air and away from this damn city. Maybe we'll be boarding soon and all of my last-minute Christmas plans will remain.

"Attention passengers on today's flight to Rochester, New York," the woman says. "We are currently still experiencing some hazardous weather, but we assure you that we'll be on our way just as soon as it passes. In the meantime, if you'd like to see if we can find you other accommodations, please see me at the front desk. Happy holidays and thank you for traveling with us."

The only place I've traveled so far today is the other end of the city. I should've been sitting in my mother's living room by now gorging myself on too many sweets and laughing with my dad at old Christmas movies I've seen a million times.

Judging by the number of people who jump up and

form a line at the desk, I'm not the only one who's considered whether the day was even worth it. The crowd has thinned out considerably since our initial boarding this morning.

With fewer number of people, I notice the mother and the boy—Jackson—still sitting off by themselves. They've played several rounds of Go Fish and War and it looks like she's trying to teach him Crazy 8s.

I wish he had something else to do. With no TV or any other kind of entertainment, he has to be going out of his mind more than any of the rest of us. Adults are conditioned to routinely be bored so when we have to spend all day in the airport, it's just another day for us. But kids still have that spark of hope, curiosity, imagination. That shouldn't be stifled, even on a boring travel day.

"Mom, are we even going to make it home in time for Santa to come?" Jackson asks.

She gives him a sad look. "I don't know, sweetie. But remember, sometimes Santa only brings what you need so you can appreciate what you have."

He nods. "I know. You told me. But I really *need* some new books!"

She smiles and cups his face. "Maybe you'll get some."

The tone of her voice tells me—and likely Jackson, too—that Santa probably won't be bringing him any new books this year. Possibly not much at all, by the sound of it. That thought alone makes me sad. Not only does this boy have to endure a boring holiday stranded in an airport, but he's also not getting very many Christmas gifts, either.

Just like Donna from that phone call yesterday.

My heart sinks as it occurs to me that I created a similar situation for another family. And there isn't any way I can change that for Donna in time for the holidays. I feel like a horrible person.

Peter called me on it this morning.

Looking around at the Christmas decorations throughout the terminal, I decide to make a change right here. The airport has done its part to bring some holiday cheer to travelers. At least as best it can. Now it's up to me to pick up the rest and do the best I can with these circumstances.

It's up to me to prove Peter wrong and shove it right in his face that I *am* a good person.

Getting up from my seat, I gather my carry on bag and set off in search of a security guard.

Christmas is going to happen for Jackson.

DECEMBER 24TH
Peter

❄ ❄ ❄

4:30 P.M.

When Tara comes back with a security officer, I shoot straight up to my feet and walk toward her in an effort to stifle the shouting match that's sure to ensue. If she thinks she can bring in security guards to keep us from having another argument, she's got another thing coming.

"Really Tara?" I put my hands on my hips when I approach her and the guard. "Bruce," according to his name tag. He has a baby blue button-up with a slick black tie and black pants to match. Buttons and tags adorn his shirt, giving credibility to his status as a guard.

"What?" She raises an eyebrow a smidge and looks genuinely confused.

Still, I plow on with my accusation. "You really complained about me to a security guard?"

"Sir," Bruce says, raising his hand in my direction. He has a deep voice that I wasn't quite expecting. "Please calm down. This is not—"

"Don't tell me to calm down!" I say louder than I intend.

Tara's nostrils flare as she glares at me. Next thing I know, she has a mean grip on my wrist and is pulling me further into the concourse away from the gate and what probably equates to a lot of eyes on us.

"Would you *shut up* for once in your life?" she hisses at me once we're out of earshot.

Bruce follows us out and stands with his hands on his belt, his belly hanging over the top of his pants.

"Geez, Peter," she says, "we've already annoyed the rest of the flight as it is, not to mention the fact that this is already a pretty crappy start to a Christmas. Let's not yell at each other anymore and ruin it further for them."

Can't argue with that logic, so I cross my arms and let her continue.

"I didn't call him here because of you," she tells me. "Get over yourself. I think I can ignore you just fine on my own."

"Then what's he doing here?" I ask, then turn to him. "No offense to you. I'm sure you're a great person and all."

Bruce raises his eyebrows in response, but says nothing.

"You see that little boy over there playing cards with his mom?" Tara asks, nodding over to our gate.

"Yeah?"

"His name's Jackson," she says. "I saw them this morning and I've been watching them all day."

"Creepy."

She shoots daggers at me with her eyes. "Not much else to do when you're grounded like this. Besides, it beats swiping barbs with you—although, here we are again sniping at each other."

"Because you had to bring in a cop." I turn to Bruce. "Again, no offense."

"It's not about—" She clenches her fists and takes a deep breath. "*Anyway*, I don't think Jackson's going to see Santa tonight, if you catch my drift."

"Naughty list?" I roll my eyes. The whole notion of Santa is not something I really support that much. Lying to kids to trick them into being good, only to break their heart when they're older and start the process of turning them into apathetic adults doesn't seem very nice to me. Better to simply be honest with them from the beginning: the presents are from mom and dad.

But then, I'm not a parent and nobody's ever asked for my opinion.

"No, you idiot. I don't think his mother has enough money for any gifts," Tara explains.

"Oh."

"And then throw in the fact that they're spending Christmas Eve sitting in a nasty airport—" She looks to Bruce. "No offense."

He puts up his hand, a sly grin on his face. At least someone is enjoying our banter. The rest of the folks sitting by our gate have probably had enough and are enjoying this little break.

"It just doesn't make for a very nice holiday," she says. "And I would like to know that that little boy is getting *something*." Her eyes wander over to him. "I don't know him, but I know he deserves to have a little Christmas magic this year. We all do."

I let out a sigh and watch the boy myself. Despite his mother putting on a smile and trying to make the card game fun, Jackson looks bored, unhappy, even a bit depressed. And why wouldn't he be? If what Tara says is true, then money trouble is a daily thing. Makes me wonder how they managed to afford two airplane tickets that got them stranded here in the first place. Unless *that's* his Christmas present. Talk about a lousy Christmas gift for a little kid.

"I don't know if we should get involved," I say, turning back to Tara. "I doubt the mother would be happy about us broadcasting their poverty for our own personal gain."

"What's with this 'we' stuff?" she asks. "No, I'm doing this on my own. I was just explaining why I brought him." She indicates Bruce, then turns to him. "So is it okay? Just this area. I don't want it to be a big deal. Peter's right. I don't want to make anyone feel bad about not having enough money. I just want to bring a smile to a little boy's face."

"As long as you're not obstructing any airport business or creating any hazards, it's okay in my book," he says.

"Okay," Tara says with a nod. "I still have some things to work out and it all depends on what the weather does. If our flight starts boarding, then all of this is a moot point. I won't have enough time to get everything together."

"I'll tell you what," he says, "if this flight does start boarding again, I'll make sure they announce it to the whole airport. Keep your ears open for it."

Tossing her head back in relief, she says, "Thank you! That means a lot."

"I appreciate what you're trying to do," he says. "Now hurry up, because the best Christmas gift anyone can have is to get where they want to be for the holidays. If we're lucky, all of you will be there sooner than later."

"Right. Thank you!" she says.

Bruce gives us a wave and turns to head back down the terminal concourse.

"So now what?" I ask.

"I need to find some gifts," she says, not really looking at me. "Uh, he mentioned a book, but I want to get him something else too. I mean, candy is always an easy option. Maybe I can also find a fuzzy pillow or something. What else do boys like?"

"Maybe you need the help of someone who was one?" I offer.

"Was?"

I shoot her a look.

"Sorry."

"It's fine."

"Honestly, though, you don't need to help me," she

says. "I can do it on my own."

"No, you're right. The Christmas season is about spreading cheer. We have someone who could use some cheer, so let's make it happen. What's our plan of attack?"

"Find some gifts." She turns to head back down the terminal. "Let's go—oh wait."

"What?"

Pointing over to my seat, she asks, "Don't you want to ask someone to watch your bag?"

I consider it, but at the same time, with the way we've been annoying the passengers all day, I doubt I could get anyone who would want to watch my bag for me. Besides, one of the announcements they've been making over the loudspeakers all day is to not touch—or watch—someone else's bag in case any explosives snuck through the extensive security process.

"No, it'll be fine," I say. "Let's go. With any luck, we'll hear an announcement that our flight will be leaving soon."

Glancing out the window, I don't even believe my own words.

❄ ❄ ❄

6:30 P.M.

"MAYBE THEY'LL HAVE some gift wrap." Tara leads me in yet another store.

Switching the heavy bag to my other hand, I follow her in. After venturing to the complete opposite side of the airport, we managed to find several gifts. More than enough in my opinion. A few bags of candy, a cheap pair of sunglasses, a travel pillow, and a couple books—one of which Tara swears she saw Jackson reading this morning.

Guess traveling through one of the biggest airports in the country at the holidays has its perks. We had a lot of options.

The total for everything we bought has already reached a hundred dollars and despite Tara offering to pay for it all, I chipped in the last of my money from the job that brought me to Chicago to begin with. You get more in return by giving to others, right?

"Ah, here we go," she says when she spots some gift wrap in the corner. "Not very many options. What do you think?"

The first thing I notice is the price tag on a thin roll.

"Five ninety-nine for that?"

"Yeah, they jack up the prices in an airport," she says. "But we can't give him unwrapped gifts. That's not what Santa would do."

"And how are we going to wrap it?"

"We've already established that we have plenty of time," she says.

"Right, but in the past they've confiscated my fingernail clippers, so I think they're going to frown on a pair of scissors in an airport."

"Oh."

"Yeah."

She nods to the cashier. "Maybe they can take the

stuff in back for us and wrap it. We could give them a tip for it."

I sigh. All of this is costing me more than I thought. Actually, money is never on my mind until I realize that I don't ever have any. Like in this moment. I want to help that boy, but you can't get blood from a stone.

"You're too shy? Fine, I'll ask." She takes the bag from me and steps to the cashier.

After some banter, the cashier takes the bag, the roll of wrapping paper, and disappears through a door marked "Employees Only."

Tara comes back to me with a smile. "I didn't even have to tip her. I just told her about the boy we bought everything for and she offered to do it for free. All I had to do was buy the wrapping paper."

"That's good. Kind of surprising considering she works in a busy airport the day before a holiday."

"Maybe this story warmed her heart!"

"Or maybe she wants to sneak in back and get another Christmas cookie."

Tara rolls her eyes. "Such a pessimist."

"Realist," I correct. "Besides, what's wrong with Christmas cookies? I know I've been missing them. This year especially Christmas snuck up on me."

"That's been my life for the last several years," Tara says. "Christmas just doesn't have the same spark it did when I was little."

"I know what you mean. I like constantly going somewhere and doing something, but at the end of the year

I just want some time off to decompress, unwind, and just *be* for a little bit, you know?"

She looks around the store. We're the only ones in here. "I get it. When exactly do adults lose their fun? Because I feel like I'm too young to be boring."

I smile. "You've always been boring, Tara."

Shooting me a look, she rolls her eyes, just before shifting to a friendly smile when the cashier comes back out with the wrapped gifts.

"Thank you *so much*!" she gushes. "He's really going to love this! Merry Christmas!"

"Merry Christmas!" the cashier calls to us as we leave the store.

Tara passes off a couple of the gifts to me to carry and she carries the rest.

"Where to now?" I ask.

December 24th
Tara

❄ ❄ ❄

6:45 P.M.

"Dinner?" I ask. Then I remember the several comments Peter has made about how much we're spending while we've been shopping. They were subtle comments here and there, but it was definitely noticeable. Despite all his travels, he must be tight on money. Quickly, I add an amendment to my statement, "My treat."

"You think we have time?"

"We'll be able to hear any announcements in the restaurant," I say. "And I'm sure we wouldn't be the first people to dine and ditch in a hurry."

"Are you sure you want to break bread with me?" he asks. "With the way we've been at each other's throats all day?"

"Haven't we broken that ice already?" I ask with a smirk. "And we've been good for the last few hours."

Truthfully, Peter's willingness to help make Christmas happen for Jackson—especially when he doesn't have much money himself—helped remind me of the kinder side of Peter. The side of him I knew back in college. That part of him faded from my memory, but now that he's here and we've been having civilized conversations, I can see it clearly. Perhaps his kindness is even the reason he travels the world.

We pick a restaurant at the end of Terminal 2 in one of the main concourses. With the late hour and the thinning number of passengers, we're seated relatively quickly.

"This is certainly not what I envisioned for my Christmas Eve dinner." He unrolls his silverware and folds the cloth napkin in his lap. "But I have to admit that the company isn't too bad."

I raise my glass of red wine to him. "Cheers to that."

He clinks his water against mine and sets it down. The ceremonial bonding ritual of adults.

"What would you be doing if you were home?" he asks.

"Home as in my apartment or home as in back with my parents?"

"Whichever. What's your typical Christmas Eve like? Is it still a small get together with your immediate family, followed by a reading of *'Twas the Night Before Christmas*, and a Christmas movie that you all end up falling asleep in front of before heading to bed?"

I smile wide. "You remembered!"

"Of course I did."

Letting that admission slide, I go on to further explain, "Unfortunately, no. Those traditions died after college. I don't really have a typical Christmas Eve tradition anymore. I haven't been back home in two years so Christmas is usually spent with one or two friends from work. I think they just invite me over because they feel bad I'd otherwise be alone."

"Oh, that's sad," he says, then quickly adds, "No offense."

"Well, the first year I moved out here my parents came for Christmas. But it wasn't the same without any kids in the house. When my brother and his wife had their son this past spring, that kind of put an end to my parents traveling for Christmas. Everyone wants to see the baby."

"I get it."

"Does your sister have kids yet?"

He shakes his head. "Not yet. But she has been making some great YouTube videos with her boyfriend."

"Is she an *influencer*?" I ask with an eye roll.

He laughs. "Not even close. They sing songs. Mostly covers, but a few originals too."

Finally, the memory of his sister pops in my head. Her likes (singing), dislikes (Chinese food). Her personality (strong, driven, kind). For a little while, the two of us shared a friendly relationship.

"Oh yeah!" I say. "She used to drive back and forth to New York to try to get a record deal. I take it that didn't pan out?"

He shakes his head. "No, but she got a job at the

school as a music teacher and last I talked to her, she seemed pretty happy about what she's doing now. She's singing in all the community choir groups, stage productions, and now online."

"Well that's good. I'm happy for her."

"Me too. I'm really proud."

I smile at him. I've always admired that he had no shame when it came to the love he had for his sister. Glad to see that part of him hasn't changed. "So what about you? What are your typical Christmas Eve traditions?"

"Church, dinner with my grandparents, opening a few gifts," he says. "Nothing crazy, but it's our tradition so I'm sad to be missing it this year."

"I'm sorry."

"It's nobody's fault," he says. "It's the stupid weather."

"Which will hopefully let up soon."

"Are you trying to rush through our date?"

"Date?" I blurt.

"You know what I meant. Unless you…*want* this to be a date."

I shoot him a look. "One step at a time, partner. We were just yelling at each other a few hours ago."

"But was that really any different than when we were dating?"

"True." I chuckle.

He looks down at the menu. Neither of us have even opened it yet. Instead, he fiddles with the corner of his.

"I really am sorry for everything that happened," he finally says. "The way it all ended. I don't think I ever apologized for that. For…cheating on you."

Taking in a deep breath, I try my best to choose my words wisely. Right after our relationship ended, I imagined seeing him face-to-face again. Chewing him out. Demanding an apology. Here we are years later and I only have one question to ask him about it.

"Why'd you do it?"

"Cheat?"

"Yeah. I mean, was there something off between us that I didn't pick up on? That's the one thing I couldn't ever wrap my head around. And it's probably why I held a grudge against you for so long. Why I was acting like I was this morning…like a bitch."

"Tara, you had every right to act like that," he says, his eyes still on his fingers flicking the corner of the menu back and forth. "I'm the one who shouldn't have assumed everything was forgotten because a few years had passed by."

"Well, we're here now," I say. "And I'm not one to believe in miracles, but it is Christmas and despite our initial reactions to each other, somehow we ended up finding a way to have a civilized conversation only hours after being reunited. Maybe it's a sign. The day's just full of them. So let's talk."

Peter lets out a deep breath. "Okay. Real talk." He pauses, then looks up at me and says, "Honestly, it was just a lot going on at the time. We were in our last semester of college. You were talking about applying to jobs out of state, I had always wanted to travel and I knew you weren't going to take a year off to travel with me. You weren't going to do anything like that until you had a secure job, which was probably the better decision anyway. I'm sure you're more financially stable than I am."

I offer a sad smile, but let him continue.

"I guess I was afraid that you were going to get this great job and move away and leave me behind. Or that I'd try to hold on too tight and I'd lose you anyway." He shrugs. "I was scared that I was going to lose you, so I guaranteed it by doing something I knew you'd leave me over. That way you were leaving over something I did and not because…"

"Not because what?" I push.

He drops his eyes back down to the menu. "Not because you didn't love me enough."

Letting out a long, heavy breath, I try to find the right words to say to move forward while simultaneously trying to process it all.

"And," he adds, "I *was* immature. Still am, I guess. Just like you said."

"Why didn't you talk to me about any of this?"

"And say what? That I don't want you to achieve what you wanted to achieve just to keep me happy? That wouldn't have made me happy. Not in the long run, anyway."

I study him. The silence forcing him to bring his eyes to me again and then I hold his stare.

"I hated you for what you did," I tell him.

"As you should've."

"You broke my heart when I found out. I didn't know

what the future held for us either, but I knew I wanted to be with you. I lo—"

I look away as I feel the lump build in my throat.

Luckily, the waitress comes back and asks to take our orders. Peter asks for some more time, which allows me to collect myself before continuing.

"I loved you. With everything I had," I finish. My eyes well up with tears, but I ignore them. "With the way you decided to end things, you tarnished my memories of us. Of you. Until today, I refused to even let myself think about that time of my life. If things had gone differently—"

"I would do it all differently again," he says. "I promise you, not a day goes by that I don't recognize that that was the biggest mistake I ever made. It might look like I have this great, amazing life because I get to travel the world. But it gets lonely. And when I'm in some strange country miles and miles away from home and I'm alone, I think about the choices I've made in my life. I wonder where I'd be if I hadn't done certain things that I've done. I wonder if I would have a more stable job. If you and I would be married, have a house, kids, a dog, whatever."

I wipe at my eyes. "Cat."

He smirks. "Whatever you want. It doesn't really matter anymore, does it? What's done is done. All we can do is move forward."

"Right."

Peter reaches across the table for my hand and I let him take it. "I know there's no way you could ever trust me again, but I would love for you to forgive me, even though

I'd understand if you couldn't."

"Peter, this is a lot to think about. After talking to you today, and hearing all of this, I don't know. Maybe I don't hate you anymore. But you're right. It's going to take a lot to convince me to trust you again. I guess I sort of understand why you did what you did, but like you said, what's done is done. That's the precedent you've set. It's going to take a lot to convince me that when things get uncomfortable or difficult that you won't do it again."

He nods and squeezes my hand. "I know. But believe me when I tell you that even if I can't be in your life as someone you're in love with, I want to still be in your life as a friend. Because Tara, I need you as a friend. I don't have very many."

I suck in a shuddering breath. "I think I can manage that."

Squeezing my hand again, he smiles. "Good."

The waitress comes back for a third time, looking rather annoyed that we still haven't ordered.

"Oh, um…" I flop open the menu and read the first thing I see. "I'll take the, uh, fried pickles and he'll have…"

He looks down at the options. "Chicken tenders."

I smirk and shake my head slightly as Peter hands the waitress our menus.

"Will that be all?" she asks.

"Yes," I say. "And we're on a flight that's been delayed all day, so we're just waiting for the announcement that they're going to start boarding."

"I heard about that," the waitress says. "I'll make sure

your order is rushed. Shouldn't take long."

"Thank you," Peter says as she turns to leave.

"Chicken tenders?" I ask with a smile.

"I told you I was immature."

I laugh and drop my eyes to the table as I consider how I want to approach the next topic. "Can I ask one more personal question, while we currently have our hearts cut wide open?"

He laughs. "Sure, why not?"

"How are you doing? Really?"

"I'm going to need some more clarification on that." He reaches for his water and takes a sip. Condensation drips down the side onto the table.

"Please don't get upset by this, but I noticed that you seemed short on cash while we were shopping for Jackson. You mentioned that you get lonely when you travel. And judging by the fact that we're currently sitting in an airport restaurant on Christmas Eve, I'd say you're having a crappy holiday too."

He smiles a little. It doesn't reach his eyes. "Real talk again?"

"I only ever want real talk."

Shooting me a look, he says, "Nobody ever really means that."

"Okay, well, right now I'm looking for real talk."

"Honestly…my life kind of sucks," he admits. "I mean, it's amazing in the sense that I have been able to travel the world and I do have these great stories."

"So I've heard." I decide to leave out how arrogantly

sprouting all of his travel stories shows his insecurities too.

Grinning, he goes on, "But it's technically all per diem work. I barely make enough to pay for these trips, my rent, and everything else I need. I don't have any lasting connections to people at any of the places I visit or even back in Rochester, because I'm never in one place long enough. I'm working crazy hours and my sleep schedule is always thrown off, which I don't mind sometimes, but it's getting to be too much."

"I could see that."

"*And*, not having health insurance because I don't have a full-time job is more than just a little inconvenient. Last year I was doing a shoot in the Grand Canyon and I slipped and broke my wrist on one of the trails. Luckily, the medic at the park was able to set it, but I had to come up with a makeshift cast to keep it in place while it healed, which I swear it didn't do properly. It still clicks when it gets cold. Here, listen." He holds his wrist up to me and wiggles it, trying to get it to click like he said.

Pushing his hand away, I tell him, "I'll take your word for it." I reach for my wine glass and swirl the remaining contents. "Sounds to me like Immature Peter is growing up. You're looking for more regular hours, a pay raise, health insurance, better sleep, someone to come home to. I'm impressed. Should we tell the waitress to upgrade your chicken tenders?"

He laughs. "Says the girl who ordered fried pickles."

"Sometimes you just need to satisfy that craving," I say with a smirk.

He lets out a deep breath and looks down at his hands. "What about your life?"

"We're talking about yours."

He wags a finger at me. "Uh-uh, no, no. You don't get to dodge the question. Real talk, remember?"

I down the rest of my glass and set it down, staring at Peter while I swallow.

"Fine. My life is the antithesis of yours. Boring, predictable, although we are both lonely. Staying in one place does not guarantee that you form lasting connections with the people around you. You need to actually *talk* to them to do that."

He laughs. "And you're not a talker."

"Not until someone annoys me enough, apparently."

"Well then you're welcome for this evening's conversation."

"Ha. Ha. Anyway, my job doesn't really fulfill me. Like, at all."

"Well yeah," he interjects. "It's an insurance company."

"Says the one who wants health insurance."

"Touché."

"I don't know," I go on. "Despite the fact that I'm not really a fan of my job anymore, I somehow spend all of my time there. Last night, I was working late to make up for the fact that I couldn't stop in this morning. I used to think Christmas Eve was a holiday in itself."

He nods, remembering.

"But it pays well," I say. "And it's hard to walk away

from that. I don't know if I'd find anything better anywhere else. And I don't know what I want to do that's different than insurance. That's what I've built my career around so that's what my résumé is going to show."

"You want some advice?"

"Do I?"

"I think you do," he says as he leans forward on the table. "I think you need to take some time off and do some soul searching."

"And you need to take some time off to stay home and recharge."

"So it looks like we need to swap lives for a little bit," he says with a laugh.

"Maybe we can help each other out after all."

DECEMBER 24TH

Peter

❄ ❄ ❄

7:45 P.M.

"Where are you taking me?" I trail behind Tara as she power-walks through the airport back toward our terminal.

"You'll see! Just keep up!"

The bags in my hands are getting heavy, digging into my palms, slowing me down. I'm getting warm from this unforeseen exertion of energy. Almost hot.

"Are you watching the time?" With any luck, our flight will be leaving sooner than later. Then again, we've been hoping for that all day. She turns to look at me, but her feet keeping carrying her backward. "I haven't heard any announcements for our flight, have you?"

"Well, no, but—"

"Then we still have time!" With a grin, she turns and steps

it up even faster. Very likely on purpose now that she's seen me struggle.

"You could help carry something, you know! This was your idea!"

Tara laughs in response from several feet in front of me. Hurrying further ahead, she turns the corner down the next wing of the airport before I'm able to reach it myself. Just as I'm rounding the corner, she jumps out and shouts, laughing as soon as I jump.

"Why so jumpy, Peter?" She smiles wide at me and then points. "We're just going up here."

"To what?" I try to figure it out for myself by looking in the direction that she's pointing to but I can't make it out.

"We need a Santa to deliver the presents," she explains, finally keeping in pace with me as we head toward a man dressed as Santa talking to a security guard. "Unless you have a suit somewhere in your bag?"

"Yeah, that's a no from me."

"That's what I thought. Now let's go in case our flight is actually leaving."

I try to sneak a peek out the window but the sun has long been set so the only thing I see is a reflection.

"Excuse me," Tara says as we approach the Santa and the security guard. "Hi, we're waiting for our flight that's been delayed due to the weather."

"A lot of delays and cancellations today," the guard says.

I nod. "Luckily, ours hasn't been cancelled. At least not yet."

The guard shakes his head. "They're not going to delay it much longer. Once it starts reaching the twelve hour mark, they're going to have to cancel and reschedule."

Tara and I exchange looks.

"Oh, great," I say. Although, now that Tara and I are friends maybe I'd at least have a place to stay in the city. Unless that would make things too complicated between us.

"Anyway," she says, turning to Santa. "Do you mind doing us a huge favor?"

"Me?" he asks.

"Yeah. On our flight is this little boy who we don't think is getting a Christmas this year at home, so we want to try to give him one right here in the airport." She indicates the bags in my hands. "It's not much, just a few little things, but I'm thinking the surprise of it all will be enough to make this year memorable—despite the fact that we've spent all day here."

"That sounds like a wonderful idea!" he beams.

She looks to the security guard. "We've already talked to someone else in security—Bruce?"

He nods. "Oh okay. Sure."

"He says it's fine," she explains. "We've already got everything covered, except for delivering the gifts. We don't want anyone to know we're the ones who bought them. We want it to seem like a Christmas miracle—for the boy and his mom."

I hand the bags over to Santa. "They get a little heavy after a while."

Santa looks up at the nearest clock. "Technically, my

shift doesn't end until 8:30. I've actually gone over a little bit on my break."

"You're not just the airport Santa?" I ask.

The guard snorts a laugh.

"No," Santa clarifies. "You're not from Chicago, are you?"

I shake my head.

"Every year, one of the train lines gets decorated and turned into O'Hare's version of the Polar Express," he explains. "I'm the Santa for the train. It's quite fun. I should get going, though, before the next train leaves." He looks to the guard. "Would you mind putting these in your office? I'll come by and grab them when I'm done on the train. Oh, and see if you can find me a red sack to put them in. Let's make this Christmas miracle as authentic as possible."

The guard takes the bags. "Okay then."

"Thank you!" Tara tells them. "And 8:30 is fine. Honestly, even if they tell us we're going to start boarding, by time they get us lined up, we shuffle on the plane, and we actually get ready to go, it'll be after that anyway. So we've got time."

Santa starts walking away slowly. "I'll be there as soon as I can."

"Gate L6A!" she calls. "He's the only boy in the group! You can't miss him!"

He gives a thumbs up and turns to hurry back to his post.

"Thank you to you too," I tell the guard.

"That little boy is going to love this," Tara adds.

"No problem," the guard says. "Merry Christmas!"

We turn and head back toward our terminal. To me, it feels like a weight has been lifted off our shoulders—certainly a real weight has been lifted from my arms now that those bags are gone.

"I can't wait to see the look on his face when Santa arrives," Tara says. "He's going to be so excited!"

"You don't think the mother will be offended by it?"

"No," she says. "We didn't get anything too crazy. At least, I don't think we did. Besides, if it's coming from Santa she can't really argue with it. For all she knows, the airport paid for the gifts. Or maybe she'll think it was a collected effort. The offense I think would only come based on her perception of the financial burden."

"Spoken like a true insurance worker."

Swinging her arm, she swats at me. "Yeah, yeah."

Taking her hand, I pull her to the side of the concourse where there's a small nook with seating that seems to have been vacated for the time being. Large floor-to-ceiling windows greet us and with the reduced lighting in this nook, we can almost see outside. The wind seems to have died down, yet snow continues to fall. I can't make out just how detrimental that could be to an airplane takeoff.

"What?" she asks.

I note that she doesn't pull her hand away from mine.

"I just wanted to say that I think your determination to help that boy is really sweet."

She smiles. "Well, it wasn't just me alone. Honestly, if you hadn't have called me a bitch earlier, I probably wouldn't have even done anything for him. I did it in spite of you."

I chuckle. "Well, still, it's pretty cool of you."

"It was cool of you to help me."

"And I want to apologize again for earlier—when I called you a bitch and I yelled at you and made you feel bad about yourself and anything else I did that was wrong—"

"Peter, I thought we said we were done apologizing?"

"I know, but I feel like I can't apologize enough. I know I really hurt you and I'm sorry."

"Well, I appreciate that, but it's time we move on from it," she says. "After we leave this airport, there should be no more talk of everything that happened. Got it?"

"So you're saying you want to see me again?"

"Easy there," she says. "One step at a time."

"Oh."

She smirks at me. "But I'm not saying no. You were a big part of my life and obviously I feel very comfortable with you still because we just fell right back into our routines—arguments aside."

I smile. "We did, didn't we?"

"And I know that you're sorry, but we don't need to keep bringing—"

My lips cut her off mid-sentence when they meet hers.

Half a second later, she pushes me away.

"What the hell was that?"

"I don't know," I say. "It just seemed right."

Pulling away completely, she waves a finger at me.

"No, you had no right to do that. For all you know, I have a boyfriend."

"You never mentioned one."

"That still doesn't mean I wanted to kiss you!"

"Sorry, I just thought—"

"No, you didn't think," she says. "You acted on impulse."

"I'm sorry," I say again, despite the fact that moments ago she was telling me how much I didn't have to apologize anymore.

"Just leave me alone for now," she says, turning. "I need to think."

"Tara, no," I call to her as she walks off. "Come back. I didn't mean to make you mad. I'm sorry!"

As I watch her walk off, I kick myself for having ruined things between us. Again.

I just can't catch a break with this girl.

DECEMBER 24TH
Tara

❄ ❄ ❄

8:30 P.M.

With my legs crossed and my arms folded over my chest, I sit and stare in Peter's direction back at Gate L6A. My heart rate really hasn't slowed since his lips were unexpectedly thrust onto mine, causing memories and emotions to come rushing back to me. Feelings that I thought were locked away forever.

Old feelings. That's all they are. Memories of what it was like when we were together and the way life was back then. Before we had real responsibilities of adulthood. We were just kids having fun. Until it wasn't.

But looking at Peter now—talking on the phone at his seat across the waiting room—I can't help but wonder if the fun times we had together is what I'm missing from my life today. Am I really happy? Just a few hours ago at dinner I was telling

Peter that I wasn't. Something I hadn't really considered before.

What is it about him that makes me act differently than I normally do? I wouldn't admit those kinds of personal details to a stranger. And after all these years, that's what Peter should be. A stranger.

But he's not. Not with our history. Even without that, our connection exists outside the confines of time. Whether it's been five seconds or five years since we last spoke, it's as if no time has passed at all. I've never had that connection with anyone else before. Not even in my own family.

And maybe him causing me to act differently isn't so bad after all. I haven't thought about work since he sat down on the plane. Because of that, I feel less stressed, despite the horrible travel conditions. Not only that, but this is the most I've ever talked outside of work. I don't really have any friends in Chicago, so other than the small talk I make at work, I have no one to talk to.

Even back when Peter and I were dating, he was always the one taking us on different adventures and new experiences. What have I experienced without him?

I readjust in my seat and take a sip of the water from the bottle I picked up on the way back to the gate. Securing it back in my carry-on, I think more about Peter's effect on me. I don't want to be one of those girls who needs a boyfriend just to have fun. That's not the life I want to live.

But without anyone to pull me out of my tiny comfort zone, what kind of life am I living anyway? Partners are supposed to enhance your life, which is exactly what Peter's always done for me.

While I'm still not sure if things between me and Peter could ever work out again—not with our very different jobs and with the fact that it's going to take me a little bit longer to deal with how things ended the last time—he still deserves an apology for me pushing him away after the kiss. He was acting on impulse, picking up on signals that maybe I had muddied up a bit. Avoiding him is not going to clear up confusions, only add to them.

Rising to my feet, I walk over to Peter, but before I have a chance to say anything, the Santa we talked to earlier approaches with a sack over his shoulder.

"Ho! Ho! Ho!" he says loudly as he steps into the waiting area for the gate. "Merry Christmas!"

Everyone turns to look at him as he walks right up to Jackson.

"I heard there was a little boy here who was worried he might not get to see me this year," he says.

Jackson huddles close to his mom, but eyes Santa with a big smile.

"So I thought I'd come and pay you a visit directly, before I head off and visit all the other children around the world."

He takes a seat across from Jackson and says, "Do you want to see what's in the bag?"

Jackson nods.

"Let's see here…"

Santa pulls out one, two, three, four boxes wrapped in gift wrap from the store on the other side of the airport. All the gifts Peter and I bought. Then he pulls out several more in different wrapping paper. I wonder if the security guards added a few more after hearing the story.

"Are all these for me?" Jackson asks.

"I'm sorry," his mother says. "I don't understand."

"Oh!" Santa chuckles and extends his hand. "My name is Santa Claus. I bring gifts to good boys and girls every year on Christmas."

That brings a few laughs from around the gate.

"Right," Jackson's mom says. "But where did these come from?"

"Why, from the North Pole!" he says exuberantly.

Jackson looks up her. "Can I open them, Mom? Please?"

His mother opens her mouth to ask more questions, looking between her son and Santa, before she relents and says, "Yeah, that's okay. Just make sure to say thank you."

"Thanks Santa!" He tears into the paper, pulling out all the gifts we bought. When he gets to the book he was reading this morning, he turns to his mother and says, "Mom! Look! He knew I wanted to read this! This is my *favorite* book!"

More laughs from around and then the small crowd at the gate starts clapping. It's the most I've seen anyone smile all day, which brings one to my face too. Making sure Jackson had a Christmas helped bring cheer to more than just that little boy.

"Looks like he's really excited," Peter says beside me.

"Yeah."

"This was a great idea," he adds.

"I'm just glad we pulled it off." I watch as the gate continues to transform from the boring waiting area into a Christmas wonderland seen in nearly every living room on Christmas morning. Between the wrapping paper, the boxes the gifts came in, and all the packaging, the evidence of Santa's visit is hard to miss.

As Jackson starts to inspect each of his gifts with help from Santa, his mother walks over to me and Peter.

"Thank you," she says to us.

"For what?" I try to play dumb.

She shoots me a look. "You two scurried off for a couple hours after bickering all morning. I knew you were up to something. Especially when you came back mad at each other."

My face flushes and I look away. "Well, I'm sorry you had to hear all of that."

"Oh, no, thank *you*," she says with a laugh. "Without the little bursts of entertainment throughout the day, it would've made a long boring day even longer."

"Well, I'm glad our arguing had some benefit," Peter says.

Jackson's mom looks back at her son. "Seriously, thank you so much. My mother has been ill. She lives in Rochester and took a turn for the worse last week so I wanted to spend Christmas with her because it might be the last one for her. We live in Florida and I didn't have time to save for a ticket and I was already skimping on food and everything to try to make Christmas happen for Jackson.

Then I needed to use his Christmas gift money on the tickets and I didn't know what I was going to do." She shakes her head, wiping tears out of her eyes.

I reach for her arm. "Hey, it's all right. We all go through things. I'm just glad we were able to bring a smile to his face. It's what we've all needed today."

"I know that's the truth!"

We all laugh and then she looks back at her son again.

"I should go enjoy this moment while it lasts," she says. "Hopefully we won't be waiting too much longer. Thank you again. You two make a great team."

"I don't know about that," I say. "But you're welcome for the gifts."

"Merry Christmas," Peter adds.

She waves and wishes us the same before going back to her seat.

"We make a great team," he says to me once she's out of earshot.

"Do you really think so?"

He motions over to Jackson. "I think this shows it, don't you?"

"Maybe."

I was so sure that Peter and I don't have a future, but maybe we do. Rather, maybe we could. He even said himself that the pay for his job is less than ideal and the traveling is getting to him. And I know I'm growing tired of working in Chicago while my family is back in Batavia. Also, if I'm being honest with myself, I miss Peter.

Turning to him, I'm about to start the long discussion

of what it all means and how we should move forward when a woman's voice comes over the loudspeaker above us.

"Ladies and gentlemen waiting to board today's flight to Rochester, New York," she starts.

I spot her behind the desk near the gate door.

"We are pleased to announce that the weather has finally lifted and the runways are being cleared for takeoff. We apologize for the delay. We will begin boarding shortly. Thank you for choosing us for your holiday travel."

December 25th
Peter

❄ ❄ ❄

12:30 A.M.

Tara and I step off the plane groggy and a little disoriented, coming from a crowded plane to an empty airport. Our fellow travelers who we've inadvertently spent the day with all scurry off in their own directions, stopping at various bathrooms, and taking different exits to baggage claim.

Jackson's mother hurries over to us with a bag slung over her shoulder and an exhausted Jackson clinging to her hand.

"I just wanted to say thank you again to both of you," she says. "It turned out to be a great day after all."

Tara yawns.

"Long, but great," I say.

We all laugh.

Jackson's mom reaches up and gives us each a hug, with her confused son looking on with a sleepy expression.

"I'll never forget what you've done." She looks down at Jackson. "And someday I'll explain it to him."

"Why ruin a miracle?" Tara asks.

"True. You guys take care now."

Tara leans down toward Jackson. "I hope you have a merry Christmas!"

He nods and rubs his eyes.

"We should get going," his mother says. "Thanks again!"

"No problem!" I call to them with a wave. "Merry Christmas!"

Tara and I both watch as they make their way down the concourse, which is much smaller—and quieter—than Chicago's. But it's home for me. And watching mother and son walk away with a smile from a potentially rotten situation brings a smile to my face too.

I put my arm around Tara and say, "We did good."

She looks up at me with her own sleepy expression. "We certainly did."

We continue to watch mother and son walk off until we can't see them anymore. The rest of the passengers from the airplane step by us as they make their way to the exit. To their homes and their Christmases. And although it's late and I'm tired and I want nothing more than to collapse in my bed and sleep for a very long time, I'm content sitting here with Tara and taking in the early Christmas hours, remembering a time when I wouldn't dare be awake at this hour in fear of Santa not stopping at my house to leave presents under my tree.

Finally, I look down at Tara and ask, "What do you say? You ready to head out ourselves? Rejoin the real world?"

She wraps her arms around me and leans her head in the crook of my arm. "Not just yet."

I soak in the moment and decide not to ruin it with anymore words. We haven't spoken much since we boarded the plane back in Chicago and yet so much has been said.

Like the way the two of us naturally sat together without any prior discussion. Or how Tara put up the armrest between us so she could lean her head on my shoulder to get as comfortable as she could on the plane. Or how we both fell asleep next to each other, without any worry about where things are going or what's been said. Pure comfort in the silence.

"Is your offer still on the table?" she asks after the floor cleaners have passed us twice, making it obvious that we're in their way.

"Which offer is that?"

"The ride home."

"Absolutely," I say. "On one condition."

"What's that?"

"Well, it's late and I'm going to need to stay awake after that catnap on the plane, so you're going to need to talk to me to keep me awake."

She slides her hand in mine. "I think we have more to talk about than one car ride will take."

With a smile, I squeeze her hand and lead her down the concourse toward baggage claim.

❄ ❄ ❄

1:00 A.M.

RUBBING MY HANDS together behind the wheel to try to warm them, I blast the heating vents and navigate the car toward the parking garage exit.

"Where are you going to stay tonight?" Tara asks beside me.

"I was planning on going to my parents' tomorrow anyway—well, today, I guess. I'll just go there early."

"So this isn't an inconvenience?"

"No way," I tell her. "Actually, it's saving me from having to get up in a couple hours to make the drive. I'll get all my traveling done in one shot."

"Hopefully the rest of the trip will go smoother than the start," she says.

I make my way around the curving road circling the airport parking lots and turn left onto Brooks Avenue. "I don't think we're going to run into any problems."

Once the light has turned green, Tara says, "Today really was a chance meeting, wasn't it? I mean, what are the odds that you and I would end up on the same flight out of Chicago to Rochester? Two days ago I didn't even have any plans to come home and even if I did, I would've flown to Buffalo."

I smile. "Must be that it's a sign." Pulling up to the large empty intersection with Chili Avenue, I turn on my left signal and get in the appropriate lane. "I'm glad it happened. I really missed you."

The signal gives me an opportunity to see her smile at my admission, although she tries to hide it. "I missed you too. I guess I didn't realize that until today—well, yesterday. Whatever day it is."

Laughing, I turn left when the light turns green and make my way toward the onramp for I-490 westbound.

"I'm sorry for getting mad at you about the kiss," she says. "I was just surprised, but after thinking about it I *did* send you mixed messages. Ones that I hadn't completely wrapped my brain around yet."

"I didn't mean to overstep or anything," I say. "I just thought that that's where things were heading."

"They were. I mean, if I'm being honest, I did enjoy the kiss."

"Me too. For the few seconds it lasted."

"Yeah, sorry."

"So what are your thoughts on those messages now?" I ask.

"What do you mean?"

"You said you got mad at the kiss because you hadn't yet wrapped your brain around the messages you were sending," I explain. "Is your brain firmly wrapped?"

She grins. "Sort of. Maybe. I don't know."

"So not *firmly* wrapped yet."

"It's just that we live two very different lives," she starts rattling. "We're not the same people we were when we dated and honestly, I have doubts that we'd even still be together if you *hadn't* cheated and imploded our relationship."

"Why do you say that?"

"You're a free spirit. You were always going to go off and do something spontaneous and unpredictable. I like structure and organization. Those two don't mesh."

"Or maybe we need to rub off on each other to keep the other grounded?"

"Okay, well let's say that that *is* the case," she goes on. "I live in Chicago. You live in Rochester—when you do have time to be home."

I shrug. "If we really wanted to be together, we'd figure it out."

"But what if I'm not sure?"

"Do you want to know my opinion?"

She sighs. "Of course."

"I think you're scared of the unknown, which is what I live for," I say. "To be fair, part of the reason I haven't tried harder to find a job in Rochester—or anywhere nearby—is because I'm scared of losing my curiosity about the world and becoming a grouchy old man."

Tara shoots me a look. "We both know that's not going to happen. You can be a grouchy old man and still travel the world."

"True," I say laughing. "But I think both of our hesitation is a sign that we need each other. Like I said."

"It's not that simple, though," she persists. "What am I supposed to do about my job?"

"You work in insurance. Find a job here. Honestly,

not to discredit the work you do, but how easily do you think they could find a replacement for you?"

She shrugs. "Pretty easy, I guess. But—"

"Think about it, Tara. If they could replace you easily, why do you invest so much in your work? Unless they are bending over backwards to make sure you have a good work-life balance, you shouldn't bend over backwards to make sure they see a profit."

"You know I'm not a lazy person."

"That's not what I'm saying. I just want you to think about how much you're giving them versus how much you're getting out of it."

"Yeah," she says with a sigh. "I know you're right. For a while now, I've realized that a change needs to happen in my life because I'm not happy. I'm just not sure what that change looks like."

I reach over and squeeze her hand. "We can figure it out together. If you want me to help."

"Thanks. But what about you? Any ideas for a more stable job than freelance?"

I rock my head back and forth as I click on my signal to take the exit for Batavia. "After college I had a couple interviews with magazines for a resident photographer, so to speak. Independent contractor, nothing like a full-time employee, but more stable than pure freelance."

"But you turned them down to travel the world."

"Right." I turn onto Clinton Street for the final stretch of our trip.

"Okay, so as an independent contractor, you could

potentially turn down jobs in order to do ones abroad, right?"

"I think they were looking for someone basically on a part-time basis," I explain. "So instead of sticking to a strict three-days-a-week schedule, it'd be more like they'd need me a lot in, say, January and February, but not so much in March or April."

"Gotcha. That wouldn't be so bad."

"But that was years ago," I say. "I doubt they're still hiring."

"It's something to consider."

"Yeah."

She squeezes my hand. "We're on the verge of the next chapter of our lives. If we're going to do this together, we need to make changes for the future. Are you on board?"

"Are you sure you can trust me again?"

"You know, it's going to take some work, but I think so. As long as we're serious this time. No messing around. If you're feeling insecure about anything, you need to talk to me. With any problem. I'll do the same. Got it?"

I smile at her. "Got it."

❄ ❄ ❄

2:00 A.M.

PARKING AT TARA'S parents' house and walking her to the door is almost like stepping back in time. The fact that it's so late only adds to it too. It's as if we're back in college and I'm dropping her off after a late party while her parents are fast asleep inside.

Even though they've long since turned off thanks to the automatic timers, I know there are Christmas lights in the windows, framing what I'm sure is a beautiful Christmas tree. A real one, too. Her dad was always insistent on not having anything artificial about Christmas in the house.

Our feet crunch in the snow as I help her carry her suitcase to the door. Tara's keys jangle as she searches for the correct one, sliding it in the door once she locates it. She stops before she turns the knob.

"Thank you for driving me home," she tells me.

"Thanks for the great company. On the drive and all day."

"I wouldn't say this morning was great company."

"It got us here, didn't it?"

"And where exactly is here?"

Hooking my arm around her, I pull her close. "We're still figuring that out, aren't we?"

"I think my mind's pretty much made up," she says. "But that could be the lack of sleep making me delirious. Talk to me again in the morning."

"Ha. Ha." I lean in and kiss her. Properly this time. Just like all those years ago, it gets my heart racing and feels comforting. Like home. And doesn't last nearly long enough.

"I'll see you tomorrow?"

"You ready to announce this to your family?"

She shrugs. "I caught up with an old friend at the airport. I'm sure they'll want to catch up with you too."

Smiling, I lean down and kiss her again. "You can count on it. And the next day. And the next and the day after that too."

As I step toward the car, she giggles and waves at me before turning to open the door. I watch as she steps inside before getting back into the warm car.

Backing out of the driveway, I can't help but smile as I navigate the streets to my parents' house on Vine Street. The day that started off horribly is somehow changing my life.

What a perfect Christmas gift.

A chance moment. A snow storm. And the gift of a new beginning.

Tristan is ready to party and ring in the New Year by kissing his soon-to-be girlfriend, Julie. The only bad note in his rocking night is the ongoing snow storm. Outside his apartment, he's almost hit by a swerving car! Behind the wheel is Grace, the most beautiful woman with haunting green eyes. She's on her own mission to get home to her grandfather.

In a selfless act reminiscent of the age of knights and chivalry, Tristan vows to get her home…never realizing they are both on a date with destiny and their lives will be forever changed by the SNOW AFTER CHRISTMAS…

More by the Author

To find more books by the author, visit
DavidNethBooks.com/Books

* * *

Subscribe to his newsletter to be the first to know of new releases and special deals!
DavidNethBooks.com/Newsletter

* * *

If you enjoyed the book, please consider leaving a review on Goodreads or the retailer you bought it from. Reviews help potential readers determine whether they'll enjoy a book, so any comments on what you thought of the story would be very helpful!

About the Author

D. Allen is the author of the sweet small town romance series, Montana Beach and Small Town Christmas.

Also writes fantasy and superhero fiction as David Neth.

www.DavidNethBooks.com
www.facebook.com/DavidNethBooks

www.ingramcontent.com/pod-product-compliance
Lightning Source LLC
Chambersburg PA
CBHW032048180726
48284CB00004B/1242
* 9 7 8 1 9 4 5 3 3 6 0 5 8 *